A Magical Jo...   ...pieces

James Mayhew

For Sarah

(who once crossed this bridge)
with love

ORCHARD BOOKS
338 Euston Road, London NW1 3BH
Orchard Books Australia
Level 17/207 Kent Street Sydney, NSW 2000

First published in 2010 by Orchard Books
First published in paperback in 2011
Text and illustrations © James Mayhew 2010

ISBN 978 1 40830 464 8

1 3 5 7 9 10 8 6 4 2

Printed in China

Orchard Books is a division of Hachette Children's Books, an Hachette UK company.

www.hachette.co.uk

Katie and Grandma were visiting the art gallery.

"Look, there's a competition," said Grandma. "What fun! You have to paint a picture like Claude Monet, the famous artist."

"Can I have a go?" asked Katie. "I'm quite good at art!"

"There's not much time," said Grandma. "The judging is at three o'clock today."

Katie and Grandma decided to visit the
Claude Monet exhibition but Grandma needed
a rest first, so Katie looked at the pictures by herself.
   "I bet I could paint a picture like that!" she said.
"If I just had some paints . . . "
   "You can use mine," called a voice.

Katie looked around, but the gallery seemed empty.

"Over here, ma chérie!" said the voice.

It seemed to be coming from a picture called *In the Woods at Giverny*.
Katie saw that Grandma was snoozing, so she stepped through
the frame and into the painting!

"That's a lovely picture," Katie said to the lady who was painting.

"My sister, Blanche, was taught by Monet," said the lady reading a book.

"Claude Monet? The famous painter?" asked Katie.

"That's right," said Blanche. "Would you like me to teach you?"

Blanche showed Katie how to mix the paints on the palette, how to use the different brushes, and how to fold up the easel. Then she gave Katie some paper to paint on.

"Now you are ready," said Blanche. "Off you go, and good luck with the competition!"

"Thank you!" said Katie, jumping back into the gallery with the painting things.

Katie looked around for ideas. She saw a picture of
some boats on a river called *Bathers at La Grenouillère*.
"I could paint the view from a boat," said Katie,
scrambling in. "That would be fun!"

There were so many boats to choose from.
Katie clambered into one and decided to row down
the river a little way to look for the perfect view.

Soon Katie found just the right place and began painting. It was going very well . . . until Katie heard a strange gurgling noise.

"Oh no!" she yelled. "The boat is leaking!"

Katie tried to row back to the
riverbank, but it was too far.

"Over here!" shouted some
bathers on a jetty.

Katie managed to reach
them just before the boat sank.

Katie rescued her painting things,
but her picture had floated far away.

"Boats are too much bother,"
said Katie. "I'm going to try
something else."

Back in the gallery, Katie saw
a picture of a street filled with people
waving flags and cheering. It was called
The Rue Montorgueil, Paris.
Katie couldn't resist climbing inside.

Katie found herself on
the balcony of a grand hotel.
People were waving flags from
the windows, while down below
a brass band was playing.
"I'm going to paint the
parade!" said Katie.

Katie ran down some steps onto the street and started painting.
The brass band got closer and closer.

Ooom-pa-pa! Ooom-pa-pa! The band got louder and louder
as it marched straight towards her.

Suddenly, Katie's picture was caught on the end of a trombone! Then, it was flipped up into the air and . . .

CRASH! Her picture was smashed between two cymbals . . .

And before Katie could catch it, her picture disappeared into a tuba!

"Good grief!" said Katie, as the band marched off through the crowds. "I need to find a nice, quiet picture with no one in it."
So, she ran back up the hotel steps and into the gallery.

Katie looked around and spotted a lovely painting called *Path Through the Poppies.*

"What could go wrong there?" she said, as she clambered through the frame.

Katie skipped through the field of poppies and started to paint. It was so peaceful listening to birdsong and the gentle mooing of a cow.

"Hmmm, it's rather a large cow . . . and it has very big horns. Hang on!" Katie gasped. "That's not a cow – it's a bull!"

Suddenly, she remembered she
was wearing a red coat.
"Bulls hate red!" she wailed.

The bull started chasing Katie,
snorting as he ran!

Katie took a flying leap and
jumped into the gallery.

"Phew!" said Katie.
She looked back to see her painting
stuck on one of the bull's horns!
"You can keep it!" she laughed.

But time was ticking by, and Katie saw
it was nearly three o'clock.

"I'll have one last try," she said.

The nearest Monet picture was called
The Waterlily Pond.

"Here goes!" said Katie, climbing inside.

Katie saw she was in a beautiful garden.
"No boats, no brass bands, no bulls.
Perfect!" said Katie.
"Ribbit," said a frog.
"Hello, Frog!" said Katie. "Keep still
and I'll put you in my painting."

Katie started painting but the frog leapt away across the lily pads, chasing a dragonfly.

"Come back!" called Katie, trying to follow him.

But Katie couldn't move – her feet were stuck in the mud!

She fell down with a splat, and her picture fluttered into the pond.

"Oh, I give up," said Katie, picking up the pond-soaked picture. "Painting like Monet is just too hard!"

She gathered everything up and went back into the gallery, where she returned the painting things to Blanche.

"Ma chérie!" said Blanche, holding up Katie's soggy picture. "That is beautiful."

Katie saw that the paints had smudged together and her picture did look good!

"I'm just in time for the competition!" said Katie. "Thanks for the paints and the art lesson."

Katie dashed to where the judging was taking place.

"A waterlily pond!" exclaimed the judges when they saw her picture. "It's just like Monet. You win first prize!"

They presented Katie with a lovely set of paints.

"Oh, thank you," said Katie. "I'll have lots of fun with these!"

"What a wonderful painting," said Grandma, when Katie showed her the picture. "How did you do it?"

"Well, I had a sort of lesson," said Katie. "Would you like me to teach you?"

"That would be nice," said Grandma, "but let's go and have a piece of cake first."

And so they did.

 # More about Monet

Claude Oscar Monet (1840-1926) studied art in Paris. He and his artist friends painted very quickly, capturing an impression of a fleeting moment in time. Because of this, they were called 'The Impressionists'. At first, people thought Monet's pictures looked messy and unfinished and so his work wasn't very popular, but in time he received great respect for his beautiful and unusual paintings, which are now worth millions of pounds.

IN THE WOODS AT GIVERNY: BLANCHE HOSCHEDE AT HER EASEL WITH SUZANNE HOSCHEDE READING (1887)

 The two sisters in this painting became Claude Monet's stepdaughters when he married their mother, Alice. Claude regularly gave Blanche art lessons and she became an important painter in her own right. This painting now hangs in the Los Angeles County Museum of Art.

BATHERS AT LA GRENOUILLERE (1869)

 This painting has strong brush strokes but still creates the impression of a light, sunny day by a river. Claude Monet made the shadows dark so the sunlight looks very bright. This painting is in the National Gallery in London.

THE RUE MONTORGUEIL, PARIS, CELEBRATION OF JUNE 30th (1878)

 Claude Monet has managed to make it look like all the flags are really moving with his quick brush strokes! The painting shows the closing celebration of a big festival in Paris. This painting is in the Musée d'Orsay in Paris.

PATH THROUGH THE POPPIES, ILE SAINT-MARTIN, VETHEUIL (1880)

 Claude Monet lived at Vetheuil, Paris, for some time and painted many beautiful landscapes showing countryside filled with wild flowers like the poppies in this painting. This picture is now in the Metropolitan Museum of Art in New York.

THE WATERLILY POND (1899)

 Claude Monet loved painting gardens, and his garden at Giverny is now a special Monet museum. The water lilies and the bridge are still there today. He painted many pictures of the bridge over the pond, at different times of the day, in different light. This one is in the National Gallery in London.

Although Katie painted on paper, artists like Claude Monet usually painted on a canvas stretched over a wooden frame and used oil paints to create their masterpieces. Monet painted hundreds of wonderful pictures which are in galleries all over the world. Why not see if your nearest gallery has a painting by the magnificent Claude Monet?

Acknowledgements:

In the Woods at Giverny: Blanche Hoschedé at her Easel with Suzanne Hoschedé Reading, 1887 (oil on canvas), Monet, Claude (1840-1926)/Los Angeles County Museum of Art, CA, USA/The Bridgeman Art Library; Bathers at La Grenouillère, 1869 (oil on canvas), Monet, Claude (1840-1926)/National Gallery, London, UK/The Bridgeman Art Library; The Rue Montorgueil, Paris, Celebration of June 30th, 1878 (oil on canvas), Monet, Claude (1840-1926)/Musée d'Orsay, Paris, France/Lauros/Giraudon/The Bridgeman Art Library; Path Through the Poppies, Ile Saint-Martin, Vetheuil, 1880 (oil on canvas), Monet, Claude (1840-1926)/Metropolitan Museum of Art, New York, USA/The Bridgeman Art Library; The Waterlily Pond, 1899 (oil on canvas), Monet, Claude (1840-1926)/National Gallery, London, UK/The Bridgeman Art Library.